BAZ & BENZ

Heidi McKinnon

Simon & Schuster Books for Young Readers
New York   London   Toronto   Sydney   New Delhi

Benz, are we friends?

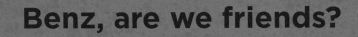

Yes, Baz, we are bestest friends.

For how long?

Forever and ever.

What if I turned purple?

That would be funny.
But I won't be your friend.

**What if I turned purple
and had spots?**

That would be REALLY funny!

**What if I said MEEP
all the time?**

That would be annoying.

Meep!

Meep! Meep!

mmeeeEEP!

MEEP! MEEP! MEEP!

MEEP!

That would be

reaLLy
annoying!

MEEP!

Stop.

What if I disappeared?

Then I would be sad
and miss you a lot.

What if I came back
and I was a bat?

A bat?

Yes. A really

SCARY
bat!

With very sharp claws.

Then I would be

reaLLy
afraiD!

But I would still be your friend. . . .

Forever and ever.

Because you are you.

For Ava

SIMON & SCHUSTER BOOKS FOR YOUNG READERS

An imprint of Simon & Schuster Children's Publishing Division

1230 Avenue of the Americas, New York, New York 10020

Copyright © 2019 by Heidi McKinnon

Originally published in Australia in 2019 by Allen & Unwin

First US edition August 2020

SIMON & SCHUSTER BOOKS FOR YOUNG READERS is a trademark of Simon & Schuster, Inc.

For information about special discounts for bulk purchases, please contact Simon & Schuster

Special Sales at 1-866-506-1949 or business@simonandschuster.com.

The Simon & Schuster Speakers Bureau can bring authors to your live event.

For more information or to book an event, contact the Simon & Schuster Speakers Bureau

at 1-866-248-3049 or visit our website at www.simonspeakers.com.

Book design by Tom Daly

The text for this book was set in Gotham.

The illustrations for this book were rendered in ink and brush, then Photoshop.

Manufactured in China

0620 SCP

First Edition

2 4 6 8 10 9 7 5 3 1

CIP data for this book is available from the Library of Congress.

ISBN 978-1-5344-6802-3

ISBN 978-1-5344-6803-0 (eBook)